This is a tale with two endings - one sad, the other happy.

The tale is about the best carpenter that has ever lived. In fact he is probably better than any carpenter that will ever come after him. His name is Carpenter MacPheigh.

BLACKIE CHILDREN'S BOOKS

Published by the Penguin Group
Penguin Books Ltd, 27 Wrights Lane, London W8 5TZ, England
Penguin Books USA Inc., 375 Hudson Street, New York, New York 10014, USA
Penguin Books Australia Ltd, Ringwood, Victoria, Australia
Penguin Books Canada Ltd, 10 Alcorn Avenue, Toronto, Ontario, Canada M4V 3B2
Penguin Books (NZ) Ltd, 182-190 Wairau Road, Auckland 10, New Zealand

Penguin Books Ltd, Registered Offices: Harmondsworth, Middlesex, England

First published 1994 by Blackie Children's Books
10 9 8 7 6 5 4 3 2 1

First edition

Copyright © 1994 Mairi Hedderwick

The moral right of the author and illustrator has been asserted

Made and printed by Proost N.V., Belguim

A CIP catalogue record for this book is available from the British Library

ISBN 0 216 94022 2

A SCOTTISH FOLK TALE

The Tale of Carpenter MacPheigh

RETOLD BY MAIRI HEDDERWICK

BLACKIE CHILDREN'S BOOKS

Carpenter MacPheigh lived on the west coast of Scotland by the shores of Loch Gilp. He was a peaceful man who loved his work. Whether it was a porridge spirtle or an oak cabinet he worked slowly and carefully, never rushing.

"There is always another day," he would say as the sun set over the hills and the lochs and the islands to the west. Carpenter MacPheigh loved making all kinds of things out of wood, but what he liked making best of all was boats. All his boats were simple in design but were always strong and safe.

Every fisherman worth his salt wanted a MacPheigh built boat.

Carpenter MacPheigh had an apprentice called Gillie Callum.

"Learn all you can and you might end up famous one day, too," Gillie Callum's mother had said as he set off for his first day at the workshop. "A master craftsman like Carpenter MacPheigh will be very strict," she added.

But to Gillie Callum's surprise, Carpenter MacPheigh treated him like an equal. All day long they chatted together as they worked side by side. Carpenter MacPheigh would ask Gillie Callum what he thought of this or that design, and where should the handle go on this drawer, and what about more of a curve on the gunwale of that boat. The days passed by very happily.

Meanwhile, Carpenter MacPheigh's fame was spreading far and wide, until finally it reached the ears of the carpenters of Lochlann.

The carpenters of Lochlann were always bragging and showing off. Instead of making things slowly and carefully they created fantastic items that looked magnificent but never worked properly, and usually fell to bits. Then they all blamed each other and a fight would start up which they really quite enjoyed.

When they heard about the skill of Carpenter MacPheigh they were outraged.

'Who does this MacPheigh think he is?' somebody shouted.

'*We're* the best carpenters in all the wide world!' shouted somebody else.

'Let's go and sort this man MacPheigh out once and for all, eh, lads?'' shouted the biggest Lochlann carpenter.

They sent a messenger to tell Carpenter MacPheigh that they were coming to challenge him. Then they sharpened their axes and saws and chisels and jumped onto their boats which were shaped like magnificent rocking horses, and set off with great whoops and yells.

"They'll never make it!" wailed the Lochlann women who knew from experience what bad carpenters, and sailors, their menfolk were.

When Carpenter MacPheigh got the message he was very
apprehensive. *He* had never boasted that he was the best
carpenter in the world. It was other people that said so.

All mastercraftsmen have special clothes to signify their status.
But Carpenter MacPheigh hardly ever wore his. His gold chain
and velvet cloak and feathered hat hung on a hook in the
workshop gathering sawdust.

"I tell you what we will do," said Carpenter MacPheigh to a
wide-eyed Gillie Callum as the great flotilla of rocking horses
appeared on the horizon. "You will be the master and I will be
the apprentice." So saying he took his regalia from the hook, blew
off the dust, and helped Gillie Callum to dress. If Mother could
see me now, thought Gillie Callum.

"You will be polite and welcoming to the Lochlann carpenters,"
instructed Carpenter MacPheigh "and if they want to challenge
you, this is what you must do..."

Gillie Callum listened intently, the feather on his master's
over-big bonnet nodding up and down in agreement.

Soon the Lochlann carpenters were surfing crazily ashore. Dismounted riders, up to their waists in water, started to fisticuff their neighbours. It took an awful lot of shouting from the big Lochlann carpenter to calm everyone down. Bits of broken rocking horse floated out to sea.

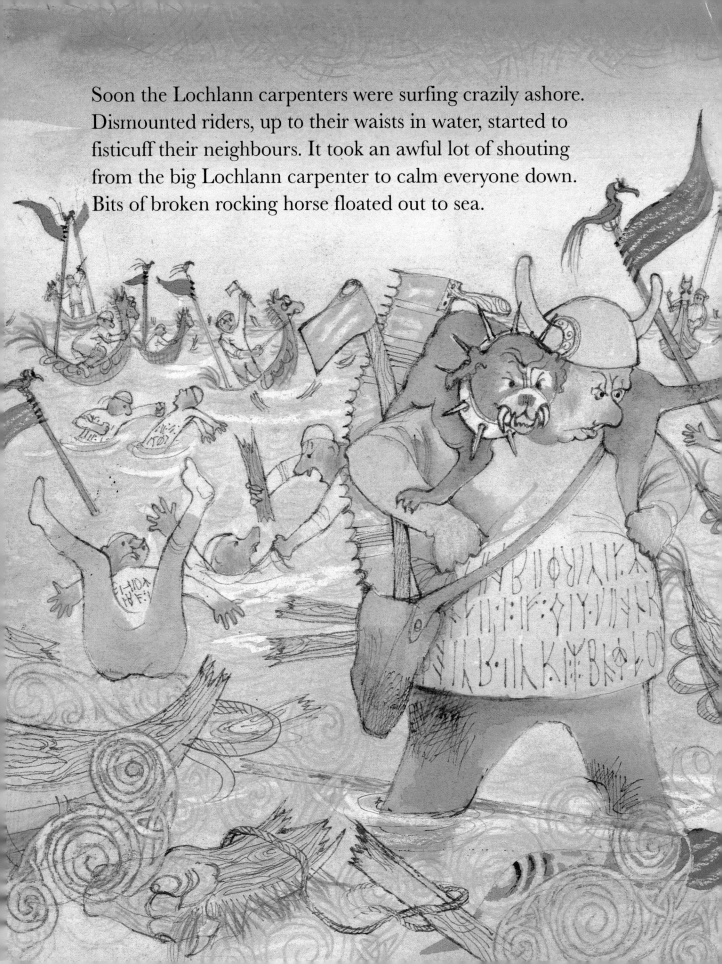

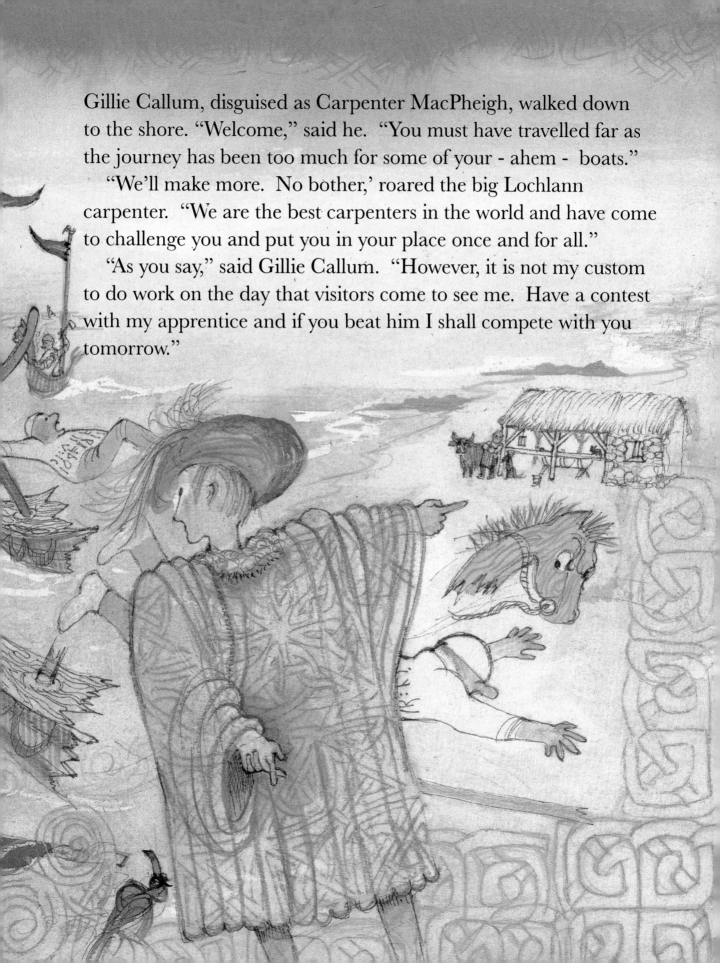

Gillie Callum, disguised as Carpenter MacPheigh, walked down to the shore. "Welcome," said he. "You must have travelled far as the journey has been too much for some of your - ahem - boats."

"We'll make more. No bother,' roared the big Lochlann carpenter. "We are the best carpenters in the world and have come to challenge you and put you in your place once and for all."

"As you say," said Gillie Callum. "However, it is not my custom to do work on the day that visitors come to see me. Have a contest with my apprentice and if you beat him I shall compete with you tomorrow."

When the Lochlann carpenters got up to the workshop they all crowded round and mocked the age of the 'apprentice' and his tools.

"This will be a laugh!" scoffed one. "With those ancient tools, whatever he makes will take all day!" yawned another.

Then Gillie Callum told Carpenter MacPheigh to put a haft on a new adze head.

"Peasy!" shrieked the Lochlann carpenters.

"The simplest things are often the most difficult to do," said Gillie Callum, winking at Carpenter MacPheigh.

Carpenter MacPheigh put the adze in the workshop vice.
Then taking a little axe and sitting somewhat apart he began
to whittle the long haft of wood for a handle. He kept looking
every now and again at the eye socket of the adze. Then he
carefully shaped one end of the handle to fit the socket. Once
he had finished he threw it with all his strength, and such was
the excellence of his aim that the handle flew straight through
the air into the socket of the adze.

"Not bad! Not bad!" praised Gillie Callum.

"Thank you, master," said Carpenter MacPheigh, humbly.

The Lochlann men shook their heads in wonder and went outside to discuss the amazing feat they had just witnessed.

"If the apprentice is as skilful as that then the master must be doubly skilled," said one of them. "There is no point then in competing against the master," said another, rather too quickly.

But the big Lochlann carpenter marched back into the workshop still determined to do battle. There an even more amazing sight met his gaze.

Gillie Callum and Carpenter MacPheigh were replacing some rafters in the workshop roof. The rafters were joined together by wooden pegs carved by Carpenter MacPheigh. But instead of climbing a ladder Carpenter MacPheigh was flinging up the pegs so that the points flew into the holes. Then he would throw up the hammer to drive the peg right in to the rafter. Each time the hammer fell back down, Carpenter MacPheigh caught it in his hand.

"That apprentice of yours is very expert in the craft," said the big Lochlann carpenter, reluctantly.

"Indeed!' replied Gillie Callum "He is growing better. If he remains with me for a year or two he will almost be as good as myself. Tomorrow however, it is you and I who will compete against each other."

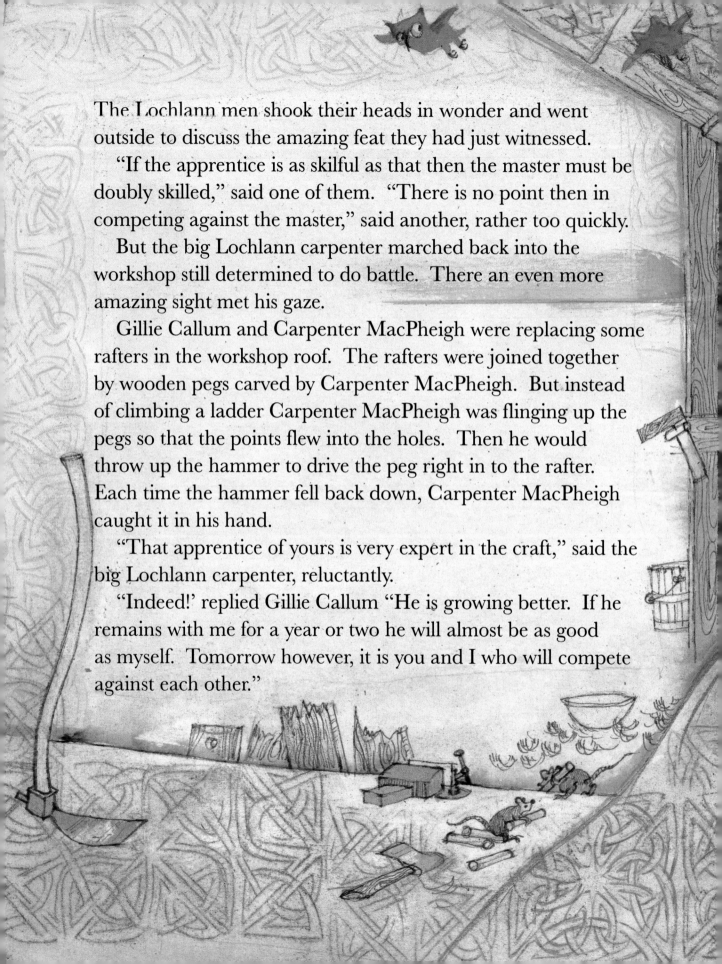

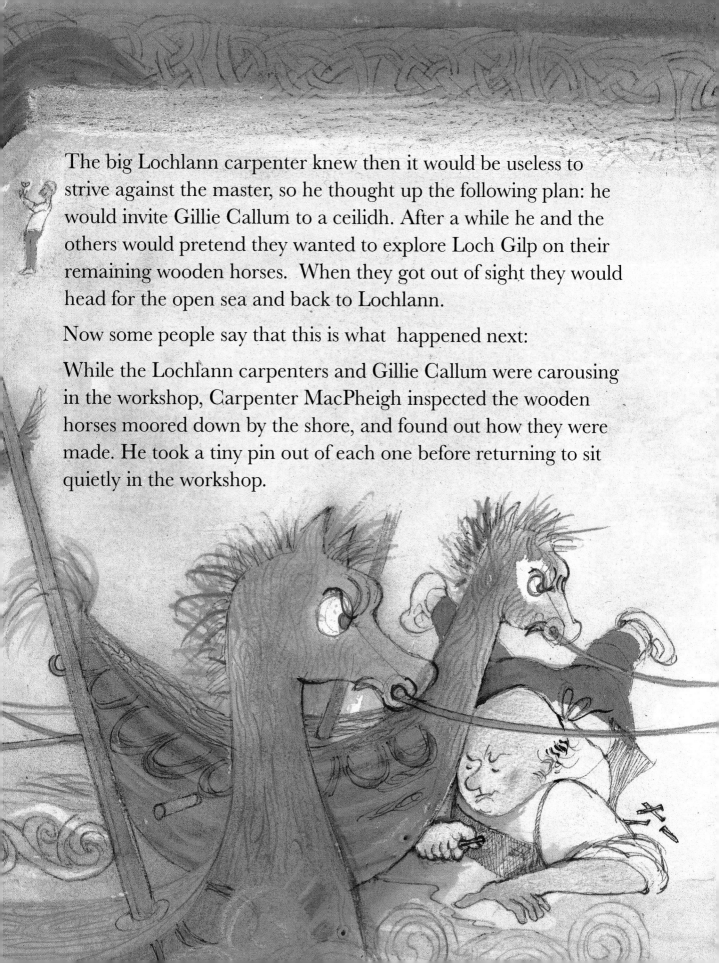

The big Lochlann carpenter knew then it would be useless to strive against the master, so he thought up the following plan: he would invite Gillie Callum to a ceilidh. After a while he and the others would pretend they wanted to explore Loch Gilp on their remaining wooden horses. When they got out of sight they would head for the open sea and back to Lochlann.

Now some people say that this is what happened next:

While the Lochlann carpenters and Gillie Callum were carousing in the workshop, Carpenter MacPheigh inspected the wooden horses moored down by the shore, and found out how they were made. He took a tiny pin out of each one before returning to sit quietly in the workshop.

In due course, as planned, the Lochlann carpenters said they were going off to explore Loch Gilp and would be back in a wee while to finish off the ale.

When they were far out to sea and out of sight, however, a wind arose and with the pins missing, the rolling of the waves soon drove the horses to pieces, and all the Lochlann carpenters were drowned.

That is what some people say happened.

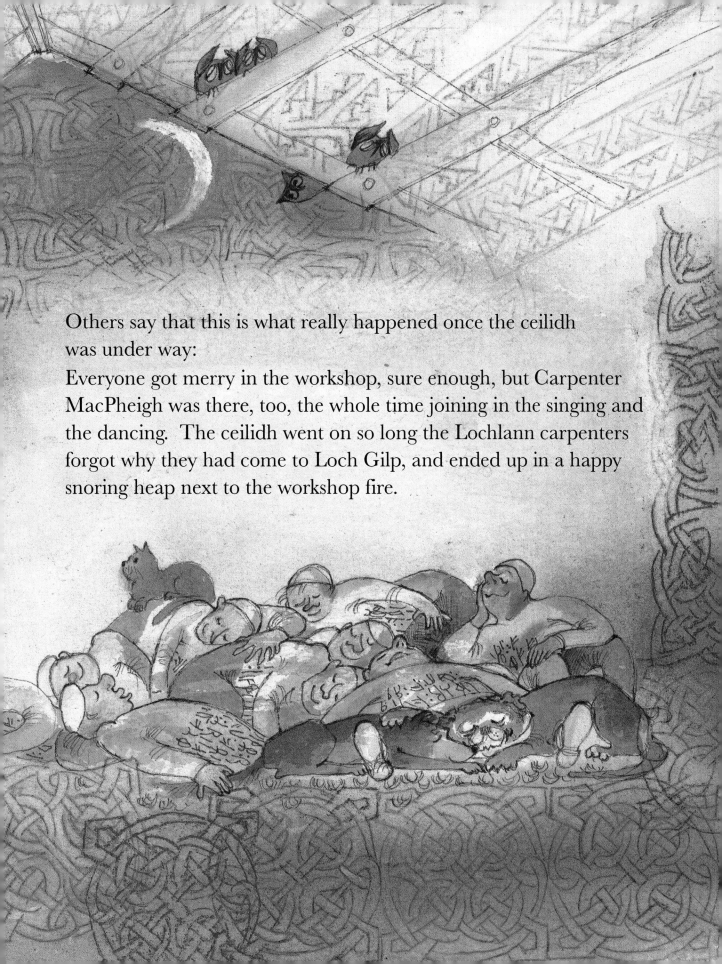

Others say that this is what really happened once the ceilidh was under way:

Everyone got merry in the workshop, sure enough, but Carpenter MacPheigh was there, too, the whole time joining in the singing and the dancing. The ceilidh went on so long the Lochlann carpenters forgot why they had come to Loch Gilp, and ended up in a happy snoring heap next to the workshop fire.

Next morning after a hearty breakfast, the Lochlann
carpenters got ready to go home.

"My apprentice will help mend your transport
for the journey," offered Gillie Callum, pompously. He was
enjoying his new position in life until the last possible minute.

"Indeed, master," said Carpenter MacPheigh. "But I would prefer to show them how to make a proper horse boat, if I may? One in which they will all have to learn to pull together. It will get them home more quickly."

"Go ahead," said the big Lochlann carpenter. "And we will give you a hand."

Nobody said a word about the competition.

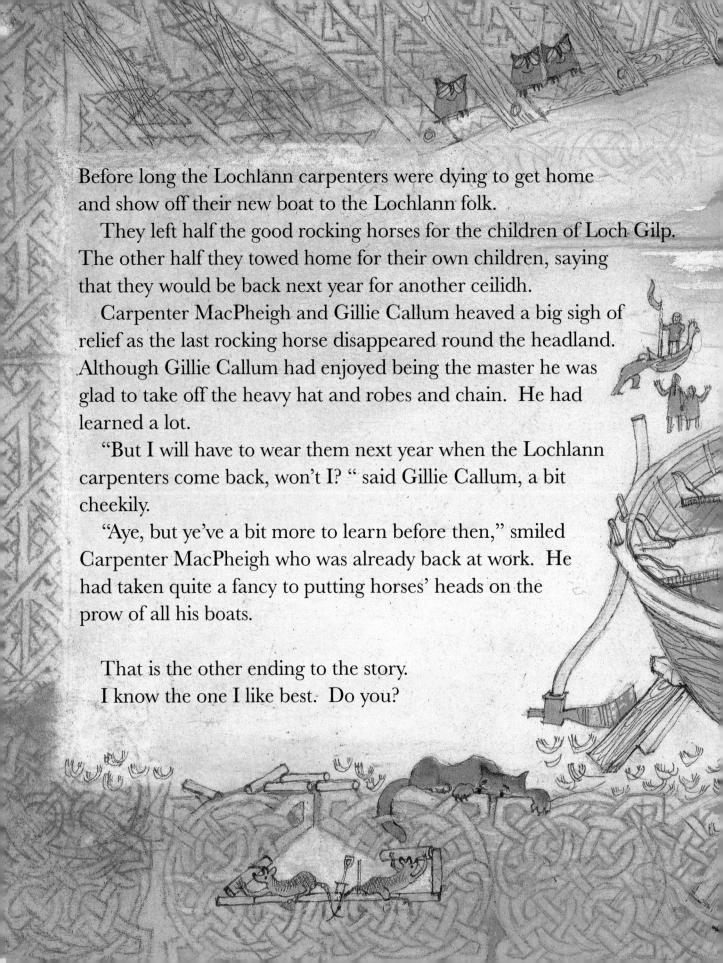

Before long the Lochlann carpenters were dying to get home
and show off their new boat to the Lochlann folk.

They left half the good rocking horses for the children of Loch Gilp.
The other half they towed home for their own children, saying
that they would be back next year for another ceilidh.

Carpenter MacPheigh and Gillie Callum heaved a big sigh of
relief as the last rocking horse disappeared round the headland.
Although Gillie Callum had enjoyed being the master he was
glad to take off the heavy hat and robes and chain. He had
learned a lot.

"But I will have to wear them next year when the Lochlann
carpenters come back, won't I? " said Gillie Callum, a bit
cheekily.

"Aye, but ye've a bit more to learn before then," smiled
Carpenter MacPheigh who was already back at work. He
had taken quite a fancy to putting horses' heads on the
prow of all his boats.

That is the other ending to the story.
I know the one I like best. Do you?